For Piper, August and Elliot and for all
parents, no matter how tired they are,
who take time to read to their children.

www.mascotbooks.com

The Sleepy Reader

©2018 David Beck. All Rights Reserved. No part of this publication may be reproduced, stored in a retrieval system or transmitted in any form by any means electronic, mechanical, or photocopying, recording or otherwise without the permission of the author.

For more information, please contact:
Mascot Books
620 Herndon Parkway, Suite 320
Herndon, VA 20170
info@mascotbooks.com

Library of Congress Control Number: 2018901335

CPSIA Code: PRT0618A
ISBN-13: 978-1-68401-812-3

Printed in the United States

THE SLEEPY READER

WRITTEN BY **DAVID BECK**

ILLUSTRATED BY **G. GAMACHE**

Jackson had been waiting all day for his dad to return from work.

When the front door opened, a rush of greetings began: "Yeah, Dad's home! Can we play? Dad, I had a Popsicle today and we sang a song in class and did you know rain comes from the sky?!" With the grand welcoming over, the evening routine began.

First there was
playtime outside,

followed by puzzles.

After dinner it was
room clean up,

then teeth brushing time.

Finally it was time to settle down for stories.
Jackson chose his brand new book, *Field Day*.

They opened to the first page.

"Ok buddy, here we go."

Howard woke up for school just like any ordinary day.

He ate breakfast.

He checked his backpack and went outside to wait for the bus.

Only this was not just any ordinary day, for it was...

FIELD

dAY!

The first event of the day was basketball. The competition was fierce as the two teams raced up and down the court.

With time winding down, Howard was fouled. He stepped
to the line and got ready...to attempt...a

TREE THROW!

Jackson was suddenly confused.

"Uh Dad? Did Howard throw a tree?"

"Hmm huh? Let's see, oops haha, Howard is about to take a *free throw*."

The next event was soccer. The game was tied as Howard raced down the field. He dribbled the ball toward the...

He kicked...it was a **TROLL!**

Jackson was kind of lost again.

"Dad, did Howard really kick a troll into a mole?"

His dad perked up. "Hmm? Troll? Oh ha, Howard scored a *goal*."

Jackson smiled. "Ok Dad, you look a little sleepy."

After the soccer game ended it was time for hockey.
The two teams faced off and the **DUCK WAS MOPPED...**

I mean, the *puck was dropped.*

The goalie stood in front
of the **JET**...*net.*

Howard raised his stick for...

A CAT SHOT!

Jackson was getting a little bothered with these crazy mix-ups.

"Dad, what's going on? Are ducks being mopped? And what happened to that cat?"

His dad answered with a big yawn.

"Hmm cat? Oh, it was a *slap shot*!

Sorry, Jackson. I'm just so sleepy. Let's finish this last chapter. I wonder what sport will be next."

The final event of the day was baseball.

Howard confidently waited in the batter's box.

The pitcher wound up and threw...

A BIKE!

The second pitch came...

STEEEERIKE SHOE!

Howard tapped the plate
and adjusted his helmet.

The...**WITCHER**...

raised her arm

and threw.

Howard swung...

It was a GNOME RUN!!!

Jackson had finally had enough. "Daddddd, is a witch really pitching? Are gnomes running around the field?"

His Dad shot awake. "Oh, it was a *home run*! Although gnomes running around the bases is kind of funny right?"

Jackson laughed and thought for a moment.
"What about.... A **BOWL KICK**! Or a **SLAM SKUNK**!"
Now they were both laughing pretty hard.

"See, it's fun to make believe Jackson.
Let's do another story tomorrow,
you never know what could happen.
I love you buddy, goodnight."

THE END

About the Author

David Beck, first time author and creator of *The Sleepy Reader*, is a high school English teacher in St. Louis, MO. He is the father of three awesome kids, who, on occasion, have definitely made him a sleepy reader.

About the Illustrator

G. Gamache is a proud, lifelong St. Louisan. Upon graduating with a BFA in Painting from Truman State University in 2016, he was reconnected with David Beck, his freshman year high school English teacher. This is his first published work of illustration.